# LITTLE
## CHICKEN
# DUCK

**TIM BEISER**

Illustrated by **BILL SLAVIN**

TUNDRA BOOKS

Published in Canada by Tundra Books, a division of Random House of Canada Limited,
One Toronto Street, Suite 300, Toronto, Ontario M5C 2V6

Published in the United States by Tundra Books of Northern New York,
P.O. Box 1030, Plattsburgh, New York 12901

Library of Congress Control Number: 2012947611

**Library and Archives Canada Cataloguing in Publication**

Beiser, Tim, 1959-
    Little chicken duck / by Tim Beiser ; illustrated by Bill Slavin.

ISBN 978-1-77049-392-6. – ISBN 978-1-77049-393-3 (EPUB)

    I. Slavin, Bill II. Title.

PS8603.E42846L58 2013      jC813'.6      C2012-905822-X

We acknowledge the financial support of the Government of Canada through the Canada Book Fund and that of the Government of Ontario through the Ontario Media Development Corporation's Ontario Book Initiative. We further acknowledge the support of the Canada Council for the Arts and the Ontario Arts Council for our publishing program.

ONTARIO ARTS COUNCIL
CONSEIL DES ARTS DE L'ONTARIO

Edited by Sue Tate
Designed by Erin Cooper
The artwork in this book was rendered in acrylics on gessoed paper.

www.tundrabooks.com

Printed and bound in China

1 2 3 4 5 6      18 17 16 15 14 13

For my sister,
Renee McGuire
– T.B.

For Lila,
who is no chicken at all
– B.S.

In a pond so deep and chilly sat a frog upon a lily,
Catching flies the size he'd never seen before.
All at once, he started chuckling at a fluffy yellow duckling
Shaking shyly on the sand along the shore.

"Don't just stand there, where it's sandy. Jump on in! The water's dandy!"
Said our frog, but Ducky only shook her head.
Ducky's mother never taught her how to paddle in the water.
"I don't want to! I'm afraid to swim!" she said.

"Ah, but nothing can be better," said our frog, "than getting wetter.
Splashing 'round a forest pool is cool, I think!"
Peeped the duckling, "No, it's scary! And I'm very, very wary.
I'm afraid that if I wade in, I will sink."

"Ducky, let me be of service! I can see you're feeling nervous,"
Chimed our froggie as he climbed upon the sand.
"It is normal for a baby – or a big-girl duckling, maybe –
To be scared of stuff she doesn't understand."

"So let's hop! I mean, let's *waddle*. There's no time for us to dawdle.
Let me take you out into the forest glade,
Where the birds are all so chatty, they're enough to drive you batty,
And you'll hear them tweet what made them most afraid."

In the sunny forest clearing, all the birds began appearing,
And they hailed the frog and duckling with their cheers.
Said the frog, "My friend is stricken! Of the water, she is chicken.
Would you help to reassure her of her fears?"

The old hoot owl from the wildwood
    told the duck about his childhood,
In an oak tree with a hole carved in the bark.
"Little owlets sleep in daytime,
    but at night I had no playtime.
As a youngster, I was frightened of the dark!

"Every night, I started screaming
    when the goblins' eyes were gleaming –
Till I learned that they were only fireflies.
Since they light my way so brightly,
    I enjoy their friendship nightly
As I bravely fly through moon-and-starlit skies."

"Brave the darkness? *Ha!* That's easy," said the lark. "What made *me* queasy
Was my stage fright – I was too afraid to sing.
Every time that I would warble for the others, it was horrible.
I would shriek and hide my beak behind my wing.

"I was fearful and grew shyer till I went to hear a choir
And the audience was asked to sing along.
I sang softly, then sang louder. It was thrilling! I got prouder.
Now I lead a glee club thirty birdies strong."

"When the skies were dark and drizzly," said the robin, "it was grizzly.
I would hide inside a cave upon the hill.
Let my feathers get a soaking? Or my toes? You must be joking!
How I'd dread my breast of red would catch a chill!

"Oh, but even if you're sickly, there is one thing you learn quickly:
Being hungry is far worse than getting wet.
Yes, the rain that falls in showers soaks the birds and trees and flowers
But at least a feast of worms is what you get!"

"I was fearful, faint, and shaky," said the cuckoo, "and so flaky
That this cuckoo bird was plumb out of her tree!
Oh, I was! With my appalling – frankly cuckoo – fear of falling,
Any treetop nest was way too high for me.

"But, it really wasn't pleasant squatting like a common pheasant,
Nesting restless on the ground for days and nights.
When a kitty cat came spying, to the treetops I went flying!
So it took one purr to cure my fear of heights."

And, then, several quails appearing
    all at once inside the clearing
Crowded 'round the little duckling in a ring:
"Savage garden snails would bug us.
    They were threatening to slug us
Every time we got our water at the spring.

"Oh, those slimy, nasty bullies
    would just terrify us fully
And would call us names until we'd start to bawl,
Till the day we said, 'Let's face them!
    Have some courage, quails! Let's chase them!'
And we learned that silly snails can't run at all."

An American bald eagle,
in a voice so firm and regal,
Said, "I, too, once had a fear," and he confessed,
"As an eaglet, I found frightening
summer thunderstorms with lightning,
Which would make me shake and quake inside my nest.

"You will notice, if you're clever,
    that a storm won't last forever,
And it leaves a treasure after passing by.
Now I wait and watch with wonder
    every time I hear the thunder,
For I know there'll be a rainbow in the sky."

And so now our little Ducky, feeling cheerful, brave, and plucky,
Couldn't wait to waddle back to Froggie's pad.
In the sunny summer weather, frog and duckling swam together.
She said, "Playing in the water's not so bad!"

In the end, when they were tired, little Ducky then inquired,

"As a pollywog, what made you terrified?"

"Only one thing made me queasy."

"Tell me, what made you uneasy?"

"I was scared to death of ducks," our frog replied.

*The End.*